This book
belongs to...

_____

_____

To Phoebe
I hope you enjoy this!
best wishes,
Jason

This book is dedicated to
Ruby, Thomas and any other
little bundle of energy,
hope and potential out there.

Jason would like to thank:

Rob for his dedication and skill and to anyone
else who helped along the way.

Robert would like to thank:

Jason for his patience, Tori Hill for her help and anyone that's
offered kind words of encouragement - thank you!

www.designbybertrude.co.uk

Bertie Needs a House

Written by Jason Sykes

Illustrated by Robert Baines

Bertie the beaver is looking for a house.
Too small for a bear, but too big for a mouse.

A house to keep out the ice and snow.
Somewhere warm, where friends can go.

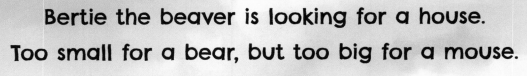

He looks **high**

and

he
looks **low,**

but can't decide where to go.

Bertie sits and thinks and thinks,
but ends up having forty winks.

He has a sleep
on a fallen spruce,
then goes to find
Marvin moose.

"I need a house **bigger** than a mouse,
but not too grand you understand."

Marvin ummed and ahhed
and finally spoke.
He was very serious.
It was no joke.

"If you behave, what about my cave? It's **big and roomy** but not too gloomy."

"A cave? **A cave?** I'm not that brave!"
And off he scampers with a wave.

Bertie runs off feeling jolly,
to see a friendly pigeon called Polly.

Polly pigeon cooed and cooed,
and Percy pigeon was quite rude.

"What about my nest?
A nest is **best**!"
And she sat down
for a well earned rest.

"A nest? **a nest?** I can't climb trees.
I've got short legs and I've got bad knees!"

Bertie's head
is in a frazzle,
so he goes to
see badger Basil.

"I need a house
bigger than a mouse,
but not too grand
you understand."

"Please don't be funny,
I don't have much money,
but some place cosy
where I can be dozy."

"Give me your cash and quick as a flash,
you can have this hole dug by Monty mole."

"A hole? **a hole?** You'd sell me a hole?
You have a mean, mean heart
and a mean, mean soul!"

"I'm **not** living under dirt and rocks!"
So Bertie goes to see Freddie the fox.

"I need a house
bigger than a mouse,
but not too grand
you understand."

"I'm starting to worry
and I'm in a hurry,
the snow's started falling,
flurry by flurry."

"A bus? a bus?
That's far too old!
It's draughty and leaky
and always too cold."

Bertie shrugs and
begins to scowl,
so he goes to see
Hootie the owl.

"I need a house
bigger than a mouse,
but not too grand
you understand."

"A moose, a fox,
a badger and birds,
tried to give me
helpful words."

"I've tried a **cave**,
a **nest** and a **hole**.
I've come so far
but have no goal."

"Help me, help me,
can you try,
to find a place that's
warm and dry?"

"So do not worry,
if you please.
For we shall build
from sticks and trees."

"A place to call
your very own."

"A lodge,
a house,
a little home."

Bertie and his friends built
a nice warm house.

Too small for a bear, but too **big** for a mouse.

A house **full of joy,**

a house **full of laughter,**

and Bertie the beaver lived **happily ever after.**

The
End

Printed in Great Britain
by Amazon